Jeff Christopherson's pa̶... entertaining and poignant story that ...
thinking. He takes us on a journey through familiar feelings of despair to a compelling future that seems both unexpected and yet strangely familiar. Jeff's story gives biblical expression and compelling imagination to those who deeply crave a different kind of church— one that is less infatuated with itself as it centers all ambitions on the mission of her King.

—**Ed Stetzer,** Wheaton College

If there was ever a time when the Church desperately needed to function as Christ intended, it is now. But God's people are deeply confused as to what the Church should be and do. In *Venal Dogmata,* Christopherson gives a perceptive, prophetic, and profound wake-up call to the Church.

—**Richard Blackaby**, President of Blackaby Ministries International and co-author of *Experiencing God.*

A fascinating parable that conveys a strong message about the commitment that the gospel demands of our lives, and the urgency with which we must live in light of what Jesus has done for us. This book will not only cause you to reflect introspectively about your own commitment to the kingdom of God but it also serves as a fantastic conversation starter with friends or family."

—**J.D. Greear**, Author, SBC President, Pastor of Summit Church

Jeff is pulling back the curtain to help us see a future where the church-as-institution gives way to church-as-movement. A future where the church reclaims a kingdom-centric ministry presence in the world. When followers of Jesus again show The Way to life as God intends. This is a future we can't put off till 2050. The time is NOW!

—**Reggie McNeal**, Author of *Thy Kingdom Come* and *Kingdom Collaborators*

The culture has changed. We feel it on the college campuses, as our usual ways suddenly don't seem to work as well. Jeff Christopherson's parable of the future church is packed with serious ideas that will help the church chart out a compelling way forward. In a post-everything world, we need the post-church-as-we-know-it so attractively depicted here.

—**Ed Kang**, Pastor of Gracepoint Church, a Collegiate Church Planting Network

In *Venal Dogmata*, Jeff Christopherson presents a prophetic tale of the death of a church and the birth of a movement. This imaginatively inspired parable helps us see the essence of the church with fresh eyes and recognize the necessity to activate all the people of God into his redemptive mission. In the pages of this parable, you will discover great hope for the future of the church.

—**Brad Brisco**, Author, Bi-vocational Church Planting Director, Send Network

On our watch, we are presiding over the greatest decline of Christianity. In *Venal Dogmata*, Jeff Christopherson takes us on a journey to find a future for the church by beautifully presenting 10 mission-critical shifts that confront the scorecard of how we typically measure success. Like a defibrillator that can kick-start a flatlined heart, this narrative of a Philadelphia church powerfully challenges us to move from a self-preservation mindset to an apostolically driven mindset where the church is once again taking new ground. Just like a powerful hurricane that reshapes a coastline, *Venal Dogmata* has the potential to reshape our thinking in order to give us a clear line of sight toward a compelling future church.

—**Will Plitt**, Executive Director of Christ Together

Just like Bunyan with his Pilgrim, Christopherson has his Luca—a messenger of the future Church calling us forward to the radical changes required to reflect Christ's body. *Venal Dogmata* helps us think through the big questions facing us: how much change is necessary, and how urgently is it needed? This rare fictional style and discussion guide is entertaining, refreshing and vital for personal or group reflection.

—**Graham Singh**, Pastor, Executive Director of Church Planting Canada and the Trinity Centres Foundation

We live in a time of revolutionary change where too many church leaders have lost touch with the reality of the world in which we live. We need prophetic voices to help us understand this strange new world.

In *Venal Dogmata*, Jeff has written a powerful and prophetic parable about the future of the church in North America. He envisions a church that will be led by multi-ethnic leadership from the margins, where the gospel is everyone's vocation, and where the kingdom of God is our only goal. Read it and be inspired to join this exciting new movement!

—**Winfield Bevins**, Director of Church Planting at Asbury Seminary and Author of *Marks of a Movement*

In *Venal Dogmata*, Jeff Christopherson gives the Church both a sobering reality check and the hope for the future it needs. In this poignant parable of the future church we are awakened to challenges that lie ahead and the shifts in form and function that will be necessary for the Church to remain true to its gospel mission. A powerful movement of new churches and missional effectiveness is possible, and Jeff Christopherson gives us a glimpse of what it will take to see it happen. This is a must read for every church leader and ministry worker!

—**Chris Railey**, Senior Director of Leadership and Church Development, The General Council of the Assemblies of God

Sometimes ideas are so big, and even startling, that they are more easily introduced through story. *Venal Dogmata* is one of these allegorical ventures. This book is a brilliant missiological allegory of key issues facing the present-future Church engaged in the world. It is a cleverly conceived, and in the end, a hopeful picture of the potential of the awakened Bride of Christ. For Jeff Christopherson, it is always about the Kingdom God, and *Venal Dogmata* is no different.

—**Linda Bergquist**, Catalyst, Author of *City Shaped Churches*

Few authors possess the perspective, background, and unique skillset needed to capture a reader's imagination of a future which rings true, yet by definition, has not arrived. Jeff Christopherson is one such leader. In *Venal Dogmata,* Jeff provides a visual glimpse into a future church in North America—one that is vitally necessary, yet far different than "Church" as we experience today. Readers will find this poignant reflection and the accompanying questions helpful for prayerful, biblical, Spirit-empowered reflection on what God is up to among his people in our day.

—**Matt Rogers**, Author, Pastor, Professor at Southeastern Baptist Theological Seminary

The struggle for the church to become something new, something healthier is really just about people; the faith they hold and the choices they make. In *Venal Dogmata*, Jeff gives us a compelling and plausible parable of a hopeful future. In it we can see ourselves and the brave choices that are before us.

—**Brian Sanders**, Author, Executive Director of Tampa Underground

Few authors recognize the power of story to teach missiology. Mission fiction is pioneer territory but contains much sanctifying potential. I am delighted Jeff Christopherson has ventured into this uncharted realm. *Venal Dogmata* guides the reader into a world of Kingdom possibilities to imagine the possible while considering the present. Want a creative resource to help move beyond status quo? Here you go!

—**J. D. Payne**, Author, Missiologist, Samford University

Jeff Christopherson's writing is compelling, but more than that, it's convicting. He extends a gospel invitation and summons for us to step into and live out a different story. Jeff's parable is set in the future, but it's a missional manifesto to marinate in, right here, right now. Jeff is a diagnostician who puts his finger on our current malaise and calls us out of the shadowlands of our self-absorption, ecclesiocentrism, edifice complexes, religious reductionism, and unhealthy marriage to clericalism. Thankfully, we are not left simply lamenting our current unhappy state because the path is lit in this parable for a fresh and full pursuit of Jesus and his mission. Treasure this little tome. It's an invitation to repent, reorder our lives around a grand redemptive dream, and pursue holistic gospel movement. *Venal Dogmata*—so good I read it twice.

—**Bill Hogg**, Missiologist, Evangelist, Director of Message Canada

In a creative and engaging way, Jeff addresses a fundamental question: will followers of Christ get on the mission of Christ? In a parable comprising characters who are ordinary believers living in an urban setting, Jeff skillfully imbeds ten missiological concepts that address four "disorders" of the contemporary evangelical church. Although Jesus warned not everyone would clearly understand his parable-stories (Matt. 13:13), Jeff's ten insights are not difficult to identify. However, his didactic narrative does make clear the difficulty will be in the emergence of a church that embraces fresh ecclesiological methods and leadership roles. I look forward to Christopherson's parallel source book that further discusses the missiological issues of our day.

—**Steven Jones**, National President of The Fellowship of Evangelical Baptist Churches in Canada

In *Venal Dogmata*, Jeff Christopherson gives the reader a peek into a world that most Western Christians fear or refuse to admit will arrive. Christopherson's exploration of the gifts and how they should operate within a culture that has long said "no" to Christianity is storytelling at its finest. The book incarnates what it means to be on mission and how that looks within a culture that has rapidly transitioned away from a time when Christendom was king. The triumph of this work is Christopherson's ability to take the reader through the emotions and hardships that accompany post-Christendom.

—**D. Kyle Canty**, Author, Send Network—
Philadelphia Catalyst

Venal Dogmata is Jeff Christopherson's parabolic and prophetic credo to church leaders based on current realities we're facing today in North America. Although the proverbial sky of God's Kingdom is not falling, North American church leaders must reconsider what we're doing today with a strong sense of urgency for the sake of future generations. Jeff is right to point us to a decade where today's church paradigm––including its leaders––is long gone and an entirely new generation of people will pick up the mission where they left off. This parable is a great reminder for us to put the mission of God above our preferences in model and to obey Jesus above all else.

—**Daniel Yang**, Director of the Send Institute

Jeff Christopherson's gift of storytelling comes to life in a parable which manages to communicate key issues the Church is already confronting or will confront in the very near future. Its message will help church leaders and all those who care about the global Church rethink its mission and practice. An easy read but an important one that will help readers discern an ecclesiology for the local church and its role as an agent of transformation in their city. As a leader who has ventured onto non-traditional paths to build various organizations to take the gospel message to the streets as I worked to bring about social transformation, I appreciated its message. May we never sell out. May we always live the cruciform life . . . one deeply wrapped with faith in Jesus Christ expressing itself through love for God and others (Gal. 5:6).

—**Elizabeth Rios**, Executive Director of Plant4Harvest, Cultivator of The Passion Center

"*Venal Dogmata* communicates a practical story on how present behavior seen in Christendom today can lead to shaping a revolutionary movement for generations to come. This book will challenge you from accepting the status quo of current Western religious practices by helping you to recognize and think through the need to make innovative changes within the church before it's too late. The book also includes a practical conversation guide to assist churches in making new discoveries about God, their communities, and themselves. *Venal Dogmata* can help inspire a church that is yearning for spiritual renewal."

—**Barry Whitworth**, Executive Director Baptist Resource Network | Pennsylvania and South Jersey

Jeff Christopherson takes us far beyond the typical platitudes of missional prophets in *Venal Dogmata*. He paints a picture of what the church could and should look like when King Jesus has his way.

—**Dino Senesi**, Coaching Director at Send Network, Author of *Sending Well: A Field Guide for Great Church Planter Coaching*

JEFF CHRISTOPHERSON

VENAL DOGMATA

A Parable of the Future Church

FOREWORD BY ALAN HIRSCH

≡XPONENTIAL⌐

Venal Dogmata: A Parable of the Future Church
Copyright © 2020 by Jeff Christopherson

Exponential is a growing movement of activists committed
to the multiplication of healthy new churches. Exponential
Resources spotlights actionable principles, ideas, and solutions
for the accelerated multiplication of healthy, reproducing faith
communities. For more information, visit www.exponential.org.

Unless otherwise indicated, all Scripture quotations are taken
from the Holy Bible, New International Version Copyright
©1973, 1978, 1984, 2011 by International Bible Society. All
emphases in Scripture quotations have been added by the
author.

Scriptures marked NLT are taken from the New Living
Translation Copyright ©1996, 2004, 2007. Used by permission
of Tyndale House Publishers, Inc., Carol Stream, Illinois 60188.

Scriptures marked ESV are taken from The Holy Bible, English
Standard Version® (ESV®) Copyright © 2001 by Crossway,
a publishing ministry of Good News Publishers. All rights
reserved.

ISBN-13: 978-1-62424-039-3 (print)
ISBN-13: 978-1-62424-038-6 (eBook)

Foreword by Alan Hirsch

For disconsolate Christ-followers
who long for a better way:
May they discover a neglected path
that leads to a Kingdom.

≡XPONENTIAL⌐
RESOURCING CHURCH PLANTERS

- 90+ eBooks
- Largest annual church planting conference in the world (Exponential Global Event in Orlando)
- Regional Conferences - Boise, DC, Southern CA, Northern CA, Chicago, Houston and New York City
- Exponential Español (spoken in Spanish)
- FREE Online Multiplication & Mobilization Assessments
- FREE Online Multiplication & Mobilization Courses
- Conference content available via Digital Access Pass (Training Videos)
- Weekly Newsletter
- 1000+ Hours of Free Audio Training
- 100s of Hours of Free Video Training
- Free Podcast Interviews

exponential.org

Twitter.com/churchplanting
Facebook.com/churchplanting
Instagram.com/church_planting

Inside

Foreword

In your hands is an astonishing take on the issues that face the Church—including the church that you are involved in—in the near future. In Venal Dogmata, Jeff Christopherson has penned an illuminating parable that takes the reader on a heartfelt journey at the collapse of a Philadelphia church and the rebirth of a movement. And like all good parables, the reader will be able to find themselves somewhere in the story and will be inspired to rethink the biblical veracity of their sacred paradigms.

Laced and imbedded throughout the narrative are ten key ecclesiological insights that are plaguing the contemporary evangelical church, which Jeff articulates in an upcoming parallel book on North American Missiology. These issues include a challenge about the lack of adaptability of our forms of church, the nature of missional leadership, and core issues of basic Christian spirituality.

I highly encourage the reader to allow the story to wash over them and then adjust the way they see themselves, their tasks and functions.

—**Alan Hirsch**, Founder of Movement Leaders Collective, 100 Movements, Forge Mission Training Network, and Author of numerous books on missional leadership

Chapter 1

New Year's Empanadas

It was almost midnight and the waft of empanadas and crispy fried perogies from an earlier potluck still lingered in the warm apartment. Thirty-one-year-old Santiago sat cross-legged on the sofa, snugly sandwiched between Luca Lewis on his right, and the red-headed McKay sisters, who were sound asleep in matching orange onesies, on his left. He was lost in thought, not exactly worried, but not excited either. "Cautiously realistic" was generally Santiago's operating mode and that was exactly where he was this evening. Deep in thought, he mechanically bounced his four-year-old daughter, Sophia, on his left knee, as he imagined the days ahead.

Santiago aside, there was a shared optimistic anticipation on this Saturday night by most who were gathered in his crowded Philadelphia apartment. Close friends convened to watch another ball drop in New York City, marking a new year. It was, in fact, a brand-new decade. The number 2050 somehow had a sense of inexplicable history to it as it rolled uncomfortably out of people's mouths.

"2050, I wonder how they'll mess with us next?" Santiago muttered. He wasn't hopeful.

Santiago, a "retired" schoolteacher, vacillated between the excitement of a new beginning and apprehension of the unknown in so many areas of his life. "If only they would leave us alone," he muttered.

Luca Lewis, or Big Luca as he was known to his friends, spoke softly: "Now come on brother, let's not go dark again. Hasn't your Father always looked after you?"

Santiago gazed downward. "Yeah, yeah, yeah," he conceded. This obviously wasn't the first time Santiago had been corrected by Big Luca.

Luca was an institution in the neighborhood. At 60-something, he had seen a lot of change. His father once pastored a thriving African American church, but that was a long time ago. Very few of the historic churches remained. Most had been chunked up and turned into high-priced condos decades ago. Only outer façades remained as an antique curiosity, something that seemed to have a historic appeal to the religiously uninitiated, which comprised the majority of the neighborhood.

It wasn't that Philly was against religion, at least not anymore. "Unconcerned" would probably best describe the general sentiment. There was a time a few decades back when the word "Christian," or worse, "evangelical," was muttered with almost universal scorn. Older folks spoke of a time when religion attempted to force its will on the country through political means—and for a season was successful. But that was a relatively short season, and the backlash was swift, fierce, and utterly complete.

Good people like Big Luca's father, who never went along with the religious politicians, were painted with the same brush as the pompous zealots and were seen by most as the adversary. Dr. Josiah Lewis, once a prominent member of the community, was now seen as an interloper, a huckster, and to many, even a parasite. It was hard for Luca to watch.

It wasn't too many years ago that it was an advantage to be part of a religious community, but those days ended quickly and without fanfare. Soon, the few souls remaining in Pastor Lewis's congregation were forced to sell the building when the tax man came to town. And did he ever come to town.

In order to raise revenues for all the new government social programs being instituted, charities that issued federal and state tax receipts for donations, and received preferential treatment under the tax code, had to, well . . . prove that they were actually charitable. To the government, charities had to demonstrate in black and white that they did not exist for the benefit of their own membership—but for the good of the community.

For most churches across America, this was instantaneously the beginning of the end. Big Luca's dad filled out all the required paperwork to disclose all the good their church was doing in the community. And they received a rare reprieve— grandfathering them back into full charitable status. But the requirements kept getting steeper, and soon too much of the church's budget was dedicated to "membership services" and their tax advantage was lost.

Big Luca still had the 2024 City of Philadelphia property tax notice for Mt. Pisgah Baptist Church. It was the first one. And it was the last one. A single sheet of computer paper with the number $68,989.08 was all it took for the historic Mt. Pisgah Baptist Church to be no more.

But all wasn't lost. With an appreciative eye toward historic landmarks, the main entrance to Liberty Village Lofts still showcased the old granite slab which was inscribed for all to read:

Witness to the Eternal Glory of Christ Jesus, Mt. Pisgah Baptist Church.

CHAPTER 2

The Doorman

IT WASN'T THAT Santiago was not grateful
for his job at the Liberty Village Lofts, where he
handled the night shift as a head doorman. As far
as jobs go, it was fine. With tips, he brought home
about as much as he had in his previous job, so
he was getting by. But it just was that he couldn't
wrap his head around the fact that he was a
doorman. He still thought of himself as a teacher.
He considered it as a kind of calling.

And he still would be a schoolteacher, if his
conscience would have allowed. For several years,
he tried to skirt the edges of the required middle
school curriculum on sex education, offering his
students "theories on sexuality." But three years
earlier, Santiago's wiggle room was stripped away
entirely.

In an attempt to reign in "conscientious
objectors," the Board of Education required all
teachers to sign a "Statement of Pennsylvania

Values" which outlined LGBTQQIP2SAA (lesbian, gay, bisexual, transgender, questioning, queer, intersex, pansexual, two-spirit, androgynous, and asexual) to be taught to middle schoolers as equally healthy and preferential lifestyles. Pennsylvania children were no longer going to be held back by the outdated thinking of religious fanatics.

For Santiago, it was a bridge too far. He, along with dozens of others—Christian, Muslim, and a few free-thinking libertarians alike—gave up their posts. Others not blemished by conviction would happily fill the void.

Santiago would often semi-joke with Luca, with a twinkle in his eye, "Ever since I crossed paths with you Big Luca, my life has gone down the toilet!" And Luca would usually manage an uncomfortable laugh. For he knew it was true. Santiago was paying a big price for his new faith.

Santiago once taught Language Arts at E. Digby Baltzell Middle School in the heart of Philadelphia. "The Dig," as the school was known in the neighborhood, was Santiago's first and only teaching post, and he couldn't imagine being anywhere else. This fact alone made him quite unique among the educators who normally disappeared for extended periods of time in the soothing shelter of the electronically locked teacher's lounge, also known by the community as "The Fortress." The neighborhood bore witness to a parade of well-meaning teachers who would parachute in from Old City, Society Hill, or Queen Village for a solid, and hopefully well-meaning, stab at altruism. When change didn't come as easily or quickly as imagined, rarely would they re-up for a second year. For Santiago though, the assignment wasn't a short-term spasm of philanthropy, but a charge that he loved, and the neighborhood accepted him as their own. He was home.

It was at E. Digby Baltzell Middle School where Santiago met Luca Lewis, and this was a meeting which would change everything for the young teacher.

E. Digby was important to Big Luca. At one time it was the second poorest performing school in the city of Philadelphia, and to Luca, that was unacceptable. Luca used to say, "A problem isn't a real problem until it's your problem." So Luca made it his problem. And, as if compelled by some inner drive, would consistently and cheerfully volunteer anywhere that The Dig

needed—and in that volunteering, seemed
always to make his presence known. Just by sheer
stature, Luca Lewis was a difficult man to miss.
Add to his size a personal charisma that was
effervescent, jovial, and engaging all at once—
and Big Luca stood out in every sense of the word.
But there was something mystifying about Luca's
essence that Santiago found both captivating and
disquieting. Through all the charm, personality,
and winsomeness, Santiago could see a calm
centeredness that he had never seen in any person
before.

He soon found out what it was.

Sophia (Santiago and Maggy's only child)
was born with a heart valve defect that was going
to require a delicate surgery with no guarantees
of success. To make things worse, the kind of
health insurance that was available to an inner-
city school teacher and an assistant manager
in a clothing retail store meant that their baby
daughter's care would be second rate at best.
Santiago and Maggy were understandably
despondent.

News of Santiago's burden made its way
through E. Digby Baltzell Middle School to Big
Luca's ears, and Luca did not hesitate for a minute
to act. He conscripted his youngest son, Sanders,

to create an online crowd-sourcing medical fund campaign. And there was more. On a daily basis, complete strangers came to Santiago and Maggy's apartment bearing home-cooked meals, envelopes of cash, and bulging bags of groceries. They had never experienced anything like this.

But there was something else. It wasn't what these people did or what they said necessarily—it was the way they did it. Their eyes didn't say pity as much as they said compassion—and love. And it was obvious, as Santiago and Maggy invited these strangers into their apartment, that these large-hearted people acted as their neighbors—not the richy-rich types from Liberty Village Lofts. These generous gifts of love were given from working people who were no better off than they were.

Both Big Luca and Santiago can still remember the morning by the bus stop in front of The Dig where Santiago asked, "Luca, why are you and your friends so kind to us?" Big Luca's usual gregarious spirit became quiet, and with almost moist eyes, he spoke softly, "Because Santiago, Jesus saved me. I didn't deserve his compassion—and he gave me everything that he had. He gave me his life. He gave me his heart. He forgave me and he gave me a whole new purpose. Now, I see people with his eyes. And his eyes always love people. So I get to love people. All of the people who have been blessing you have the same story. They love you my friend, because they love Jesus. And I love you Santiago—and your sweet baby girl, Sophia. But the best news of all is that Jesus loves you so much more."

Santiago and Maggy soon found themselves in Luca's apartment experiencing "religion" like they never knew existed. A Christian community surrounded them—praying for Sophia's healing, sharing the story of Jesus Christ, and genuinely loving one another.

Both Santiago and Maggy were on a whole new journey, one that would change everything about their lives.

And so was baby Sophia.

After the lighted ball made its way back to its point of origin, kisses and hugs exchanged, empanada pans and perogi pots cleaned up, and the McKay sisters roused from their New Year's snooze—the party melted away into the crisp Pennsylvania January evening.

"Thanks so much for hosting again brother," Luca offered as he bear-hugged his friend.

"Our distinct pleasure," Santiago said with a sincere sense of warmth. "Next time forget the perogies and bring some soul food! I didn't take you for an African-Ukrainian." Big Luca's baritone laugh could be heard by all the neighbors as he made his way down the apartment hall.

"See you on Wednesday," Luca said, motioning a wave with his right hand.

"You bet."

Santiago always looked forward to Wednesdays.

Chapter 3

Shine the Light

PHILADELPHIA FREEDOM WAS the spiritual brainchild of a much younger, thinner Luca Lewis. The name was a crafty double-entendre that beckoned back to another era, while at the same time spoke of a yearning for a future that was deep within his spirit—one-part past, one-part future. It was a very clever name. Well, at least Luca thought so.

The past part was taken from the title of an old song sung by a long-forgotten British singer. Luca didn't quite remember all of it but semi-recalled his mother singing it around the house when he was a child. The only part that stuck in his mind were a few words with a semblance of a tune that he'd always mangle in a most cheerful manner,

"Shine the light, won't you shine the light. Philadelphia freedom, I love you, yes I do . . . ."

What Santiago found most remarkable was that, as frequently as he'd break out the ditty, it was never actually the same twice. "You could be canonized as a saint," Santiago would tease him, "because it's a documentable miracle that our 'theme song' has an infinitude of melodies—all written and performed by you!"

But to Luca Lewis, the tune, and the past history of the song, was an almost insignificant detail. It was the future which grabbed his imagination and wouldn't let go.

The future part had two intentions as well. One was for broken-hearted people he grew up with at Mt. Pisgah Baptist. The other was for the city of Philadelphia itself. Luca had a vision for a movement that would start in "the city of brotherly love," and from there would "shine its light" across the entire globe. Luca was never one to think small.

"Philadelphia Freedom," Luca triumphantly whispered as if it were already a thing, "is the right plan for the right time."

CHAPTER 4

The Nays Got It

DESPITE THE COMMON stereotypes of the mid 2020s, the people of Mt. Pisgah, as evangelicals, were not xenophobes—in fact they were anything but. As a traditional African American congregation, they had long been on the other side of the issue. Most congregants had first-hand stories of how "good Christian" folks had treated them as their inferior, and much worse. As far as targets of white nationalism goes, they were "Exhibit A."

But it didn't matter. The national mood was not making such distinctions. As evangelicals, Mt. Pisgah Baptist was on the wrong side of public sentiment. Even though Dr. Lewis spent hours faithfully laboring in his study, fewer and fewer filled the pews to hear his eloquent homilies. The once thriving congregation of Mt. Pisgah Baptist continued to evaporate, year by year—until only a handful of the most faithful remained.

But it didn't have to be this way. Well before the decisive tax letter of 2024, Pastor Lewis had other ideas for his church.

Years before the majority of Mt. Pisgah Baptist Church realized that it was in big trouble, both Luca and his dad grew increasingly frustrated with the lopsided way churches operated and couldn't fathom how this could be Jesus' plan for global evangelization. "A small handful of ministers and a building full of ministry projects," Reverend Lewis would often say. "It seemed absurd on its face."

Luca would dream with his father about a different future for Mt. Pisgah—one where the mission was the community and the ministers were God's people giving themselves away to the neighborhood and to one another. It seemed a bit utopian to be sure, but certainly worth pursuing. Small steps at first, and bigger steps later, a plan was hatched that was calculated to lead to the total reorientation of Mt. Pisgah Baptist Church back toward Jesus' mission.

Luca and his father's dream was bold and shrewd and wholly righteous all at the same time.

But it would never happen.

When the good people of Mt. Pisgah got a whiff of where their idealistic pastor was heading, they circled the wagons and put Dr. Lewis's naïve dream to death with one very democratic decision:

121 to 34. The "nays" ruled the day.

Marcus E. Robinson, the charismatic chairman of deacons who led the insurrection, shamelessly pronounced in a flowery extravaganza of a victory speech that their "Almighty God had truly spoken through his people." To most, it seemed a bit overdone, but the congregation managed a display of agreement by muttering an unconvincing "amen."

And things would stay as they were until the end—which came much sooner than anyone expected. Because nobody saw the tax man coming.

So that was the end, but mingled in this ignominious finale was also a fresh new beginning. Like a phoenix rising from its ashes—and not coincidentally on Easter Sunday, March 31st, 2024—Philadelphia Freedom was born. Luca and four other faith-filled idealists from the cold, motionless cadaver of Mt. Pisgah formed an interdependent leadership team. These five, and their families, would be the only "already evangelized" to be invited. They needed a fresh start that was miles away from the ideas and aspirations of "church" that was desired by most churchmen.

And so, it was a brand-new beginning. And Luca Lewis, with no seminary letters behind his name, was to become Philadelphia Freedom's founding pastor.

Well, sort of.

You see, as a younger man, Luca could never imagine himself as a pastor. It's not that he didn't appreciate his dad's work or respect the integrity of his faith—it was just that this was something that he would never want to do. It wasn't that it was unimportant—it was just not important enough. Not enough to consume the one life he had been given.

Luca had a different imagination. He dreamed of an unleashing of a Jesus movement that would fashion a different kind of church. One that was less fascinated with Sunday performances.

One that could introduce Philadelphians to their Savior.

Luca dreamed of the Body of Christ that imitated the Person of Christ. And it was going to take more than a pastor to pull that off.

CHAPTER 5

The Way to Wednesday

WEDNESDAY WAS UNUSUALLY sunny for
a typical Philadelphia winter's day. And so was
Santiago's disposition. The pessimistic way he
started the week had completely vanished as he
rode the Route 15 trolley to Fishtown, heading to
the city headquarters of Philadelphia Freedom.

He loved Wednesdays.

Santiago arrived at the old three-story brick
warehouse that had been converted into fitness
gyms of various names by numerous owners, each
less successful than its predecessor. Then a sketchy
youth hostel. Finally, it sat, vacant and ramshackle
as if it were a monument to the absurdity of
yesteryear's ill-fated idea of gentrification.

But now it was a home for their movement.

The first floor's grand hallway was lined
with ministries designed to meet the needs of
Philadelphia's most vulnerable. Each one with
signage and environments that declared that

they were putting their very best foot forward. It was always abuzz with grateful immigrants from around the globe, recovering addicts of assorted dependencies, desperate single mothers, and adult students eager for a fresh start by learning critical life skills.

The second floor was rented to local businesses of various forms—and all of the proceeds went to underwrite the ministries of the first floor. The business owners and shop keepers took personal pride in the fact that their business was helping to do good in the community—most went well beyond their contractual requirements in the way that they invested in the first-floor ministries. It was a brilliant relationship.

But the third floor was mission control for the movement. In contrast to the first floor, it was substantially plain—almost austere. One large room with refinished oak floors and 150 black plastic chairs lined up in fifteen straight rows. At the front stood a large video screen, a simple wooden podium, and two microphones. That was all. The big room was flanked on both sides by smaller glass-walled meeting rooms—each fitted with a large meeting table, solid wooden chairs, and a video monitor.

Santiago arrived early, as usual, and walked up the stairwell steps with his friend and neighbor Campbell, doting dad to the beautiful McKay sisters, who had slept soundly on his couch three days before. These friends were both introduced to the Philadelphia Freedom movement at about the same time and in very similar ways. Their lives and their families had been completely changed because ordinary Philadelphians had loved them during a very dark hour. The bond between Santiago and Campbell was quiet but deep. It was forged through the adventures and difficulties of ministry as these two disciples learned to follow the Way of Jesus together.

Boy, Santiago loved Wednesdays.

CHAPTER 6

The Shift

LUCA SAT AT his desk and stared at the wooden-framed photograph of his father, Dr. Josiah Lewis . . . his dear, sweet dad. "I'm a lot like you, Dad . . . I have a dream too," he said out loud to the smiling man looking back at him. He picked up a pen and began to doodle as he thought. How could he express what was becoming more and more clear in his own mind and heart, in a way that others could understand and be motivated by?

He knew that his idea wasn't just a reaction to what he didn't like. He had long grown past his frustration with the Sunday-morning-centeredness of churches. Instead, his vision for Philadelphia Freedom was coming out of a new-found recognition of the spiritual disorders that were everywhere he looked.

He thought about his Christmas shopping trip a few months back. He had been warmly greeted at Patterson's Jewelry by a woman named Brenda, who by Luca's estimation had appeared to be in her mid-thirties. Brenda had recognized at once that familiar male look of awkward uncertainty that often came bumbling into her store. She politely asked, "Can I be of help?" He told her that he was looking for a small gold cross on a "dainty" chain for his wife. To Luca, "dainty" was a veiled euphemism for cheap. It was to be a special Christmas gift, and Luca didn't have a lot to spare.

Brenda excitedly exclaimed, "Oh, we have just the ticket." Then, she directly proceeded to carefully bring out two dark blue velvet trays from the bottom corner shelf. By the dust covering the hinged glass lid, it was obvious that these were not in high demand.

"Sir, we have both kinds. We have the plain ones, and the ones with the little man on them. Most are in 14K gold, although this row is in 10K. Which do you prefer?" Luca had to take a step back to gather himself. The innocence of the "little man" description cut through his spirit like a hot knife through butter. The idea of the cross was as familiar to Brenda as the polar ice shelves would be to a tribesman in Papua New Guinea. This was deeply troubling. How had he, a pastor's son raised in the streets of Philly, missed something so fundamental? How had he missed the fact that the Good News that his church so passionately preached about and so energetically sang about never seemed to make its way across the street? Why hadn't he noticed before that the gospel was locked selfishly behind stone and cement—a world away from those who needed it the most?

All that Luca could manage was a long, slow, and demoralized exhale.

Once Luca gained his composure, he took the opportunity to explain the story of "the little man" to a polite but curious saleswoman. Luca left Patterson's Jewelry emotionally befuddled. He was excited to have been able to share his faith, and yet felt a deep sadness, knowing that this dear woman had grown up in the shadow of Mt. Pisgah's steeple and had absolutely no perspective on the very subject that should have been his church's mission.

As he leaned back at his desk and recollected that encounter, he realized that something had shifted in his soul while Christmas shopping that day.

And it would stay shifted.

"Disorder #1: The spiritual limitations of the people in our community," he wrote in big block letters. He was convinced that most people in his community had no axe to grind when it came to the gospel. They were simply totally unaware of the true Christian message. *How many more Brendas are out there?* he contemplated. *Neighbors who have not rejected the Good News of Jesus—they simply haven't heard?* Luca was fully convinced that it wasn't Brenda's responsibility to seek out a church. It was the church's responsibility to go and find the Brendas.

But will the church? Do they even want to? he wondered. *Do we really care in the first place?* He knew the true answer, which led him to the next disorder:

"Disorder #2: Malaise in the church," he slowly wrote.

Sure, most churches could work up some emotion and manufacture some passion within the walls of the building during the appointed worship hour—but then what? Why did it almost never translate into gospel action? Why did it seem so put on?

He put down his pen and leaned back in his old chair. He knew why. He had seen it all his life—in fact, he had had a front row seat to the source of the problem. There was no action beyond the Sunday spectacular because the gospel wasn't really anybody's responsibility, except for the pastor's. They paid him for that. Plumbers don't ask the pastor to snake toilets; mechanics don't ask pastors to change crank shafts; and pastors should take care of the religion business and let plumbers plumb and mechanics twist wrenches. Certainly, nobody would state it quite so crassly, but he knew that was the general sentiment. No one saw the gospel as their job. It was hired out. And that was a problem.

The Big Idea.

He wrote those three words with deliberate strokes and a determined expression on his face. Luca's big idea was that the gospel would be everyone's mission. All Joes and no pros. Plumbers and mechanics and schoolteachers and accountants all had a mission. They had a gospel responsibility. In fact, they had two vocations: one to put bread on the table and the other to serve their community in the name and power and authority of Jesus Christ. Co-vocations that synced together as a singular kingdom-centered parish.

Luca could already imagine the kingdom punch. And it made him smile.

However, thoughts of Mt. Pisgah Baptist Church reminded him that there was an additional limitation to any future movement.

"Disorder #3: The circular logic of how most churches operate," he added to his list.

If the gospel is going to hit the streets instead of lingering in safe sanctuaries, then churches will have to organize leadership around that gospel mission and not simply around Sunday services. There would always be a shepherding function to care for the needs of those in distress—but that would be only one of several roles required for a missionary advance.

He scribbled a random design around the edges of the paper while he thought about what needed to happen. To Luca, internal preoccupations had long proven ineffective for external advance. Luca would unleash Philadelphia Freedom through a diverse leadership team, who together would resemble the person and ministry of Jesus Christ. Just as Jesus was all at once a missionary, a prophet, an evangelist, a good shepherd, and a teacher, so too his body on earth should embody these functions. At least if Luca had his way. Ephesians 4:1-16 would become their constitution.

Luca leaned back again and recalled his dad's growing frustration with Mt. Pisgah in the days leading up to the big vote. One sermon in particular was as vivid in Luca's memory as the day it was preached. He remembered his dad walking to the pulpit to preach from this text, and he introduced it saying, "Today, I am going to show you from God's Holy Word how the church of Jesus Christ has become, in our day, an impotent, frivolous, irrelevant religious institution, instead of its rightful posture of being the most powerful influence for good in the world—the influence that it was designed from all eternity to wield."

From there, Dr. Josiah Lewis traced back through the past decades of church history how things had become undone. He started by expounding on God's eternal intentions for his church. He preached, "Apostolic leaders are our missionaries. They think mission. They plant churches that think mission. The prophets among us keep things honest. They filter everything through two questions: "Is this in line with God's Word?" and, "Is this in line with what God has asked of us?" The evangelists create an engaging culture with the outside world. They recruit the new kingdom troops. And the shepherds care for the needs of the flock. And the teachers make sure that everyone is theologically grounded. You see, God's plan is designed for movement!"

Luca remembered that the congregation seemed to be in agreement with his dad to this point of the message, with hearty "Amens" and "Preach" and "Say So's" generously and frequently offered.

But then Pastor Lewis began to meddle.

"But what has happened? Why do we not see this apostolic-missionary impulse present in the very church today that claims to bear Jesus' name?"

"I'll tell you why!" he said with the conviction and authority of a man who had just come down from a holy mountain. "It is not because we are theologically confused by differences between offices and functions. It is not because we do not understand that the Body of Christ is supposed to function with the same priorities as the Person of Christ. It is only because we have become a very selfish people."

From this point of the message onward, the "Amens" and "Uh-huhs" were no longer a thing. The room was still and quiet. But Luca's dad did not relent.

"Missionaries think mission," he shouted. "But the ninety and nine safe sheep in the fancy air-conditioned sheep pen cry, 'meee, meee.' And they do not stop. So the apostolic leaders grow tired and frustrated and exasperated and weary with the unwillingness of the self-absorbed church to join Christ in his redemptive mission. And so they leave.

"Now the church no longer has a compelling mission. So the prophets have nothing to do. So they leave.

"And with the prophets gone, the evangelists have nobody to keep them honest, so they do anything to get a sale. 'Raise your hand if you want to go to heaven!' Can I get a witness?"

But no witness was to be found. Only more silence.

Pastor Lewis, dramatically slowing his cadence, hunched over and whispered into the microphone, "And this leaves the shepherds and the teachers to care for, and attempt to disciple, a largely un-re-gen-er-ate congregation."

And then Dr. Lewis grew quiet. With both elbows on the mahogany pulpit, clasping his hands together with closed eyes, he said softly, "Beloved, this history that I have just described is the very history of Mt. Pisgah Baptist Church.

Seventy-six years previously, we started as an inner-city rescue mission under the courageous and apostolic leadership of the Reverend Isaiah Townsend. But look what we have become today. Now, we have to have a vote on whether or not we will be a selfish, self-centered, self-consumed people."

Memories like this do not easily fade away. For Luca, this one moment cemented his resolve and prepared his spirit for a new life that lay in front of him.

And it would be a big life.

Luca thumbed through the tattered pages of his well-worn Bible and poured over the text once again. As he read, deep emotions rose to the surface. He was a flummoxed conglomeration of both excitement and frustration all at once. Excited about what could be. What was going to be. And aggravated by what had been. Because it didn't have to be. If only Mt. Pisgah had had the courage and conviction to represent the mission of Christ instead of the conveniences of their precious status quo. If only . . . .

But then his frustration gave way to a profound, singular feeling of excitement. A broad smile grew across Luca's face that turned his eyes into narrow, deep slits. "We're going to do this dad," he said with a quiet conviction. "We are going to do this."

Then Luca leaned back in his chair once again and read out loud to the familiar, loving, and sympathetic face that was always smiling back at him:

> I therefore, a prisoner for the Lord, urge you to walk in a manner worthy of the calling to which you have been called, with all humility and gentleness, with patience, bearing with one another in love, eager to maintain the unity of the Spirit in the bond of peace. There is one body and one Spirit—just as you were called to the one hope that belongs to your call— one Lord, one faith, one baptism, one God and Father of all, who is over all and through all and in all. But grace was given to each one of us according to the measure of Christ's gift . . . And he gave the apostles, the prophets, the evangelists, the shepherds and teachers, to equip the saints for the work of ministry, for building up the body of Christ, until we all attain to the unity of the faith and of the knowledge of the Son of God, to mature manhood, to the measure of the stature of

the fullness of Christ, so that we may no longer be children, tossed to and fro by the waves and carried about by every wind of doctrine, by human cunning, by craftiness in deceitful schemes. Rather, speaking the truth in love, we are to grow up in every way into him who is the head, into Christ, from whom the whole body, joined and held together by every joint with which it is equipped, when each part is working properly, makes the body grow so that it builds itself up in love.[1]

It was all so obvious to Luca. He knew what he must do next. He had to flesh out role descriptions, responsibilities, and the characteristics of the people who would fill them. He would describe it as "a diverse co-vocational leadership team unleashed for kingdom revelation outside the safety of church walls." The thought gave him goosebumps already.

First, though, he had to finish this list. The fourth and final disorder, as he saw it, was "the problem of corporate gravitational pull." Looking at the words he had just written brought to his mind the decision-making process that Mt.

---

1. Ephesians 4:1-7; 11-16 (ESV)

Pisgah Baptist's leadership had always used. Every decision was made based on a single criterion, "Would this be good for the church?" It had seemed obvious to Luca that to the Board of Mt. Pisgah Baptist Church God's will was always the option that protected the church from exercising faith. His church's motto might just as well have been ripped off Bowman's Construction's billboards which broadcasted in bold letters, *"Safety First!"*

To Luca, playing it safe was the very antithesis of following Christ—yet it seemed to be the only impulse that guided Mt. Pisgah. Even though Jesus spoke of the spiritual death mingled in the activity of "saving ourselves," looking back, it seemed to him that his "churchmanship" was discipling him to be anything but a follower of Jesus. "To follow Jesus," Luca pondered, "You have to go somewhere!" Luca could see through the smokescreen of the flowery spiritual language that rechristened *darkness* to the more palatable terms of *corporate stewardship* and *sustainability*— and he wasn't fooled. Though the obfuscation may have bamboozled many, it did not dupe Luca. His dad had showed him many times over that the shell game had always been rigged in favor of the house.

He chuckled to himself as he remembered the day that he had cheekily said to his dad after an exhausting covenant membership meeting, "Say what you want dad, but darkness is what darkness does." His father, always the teacher, replied with a wink and yet a slightly corrective tone, "I think you mean, 'A rose by any another name would smell as sweet.'" To which Luca swiftly blurted, "Or, more fittingly dad, 'A pile of purse-poodle poo plopped in a Chestnut Street Gucci bag—still stinketh to high heaven!'"

They both bent over in cathartic laughter and howled until tears ran down their faces. "Sh-Shakesp-Shakespeare had never been quite so . . . eloquent son," Luca's dad managed to stammer, desperately trying to regain composure.

There had been some good memories.

Now, looking ahead to the challenges to come, it seemed to Luca that the gravitational pull toward corporate security was almost impossible to overcome. It was linked too deeply to our fallen selves. So he would have to structurally de-link it from the problem of baser natures by rejecting self-saving "addition" and instead answer the self-sacrificial call to "multiplication."

He was craving some coffee. The last thing he added to his well-doodled page was the phrase that he knew would change his life. It would in fact change everything: *"I will lead a growing group of friends who will give themselves away for the sake of the kingdom of God."*

Luca Lewis had a dream.

Chapter 7

Venal Dogmata

BEFORE THE BIG vote at Mt. Pisgah Baptist, the days when Pastor Lewis still had a fire in his spirit, Luca and his father spoke often of a different kind of church. One that looked more like the one you could more easily imagine in book of Acts than you could in its European shadow that was the updated and exported West. Although Dr. Lewis was an educated man, with an undergraduate degree from Cairn University and two graduate degrees from Westminster Theological Seminary, he did not make a big deal of it. He spoke plainly in a way that most everyone in his community could appreciate and understand.

Well, usually.

Luca remembered like it was yesterday the day his dad passed around a photocopied and hand-stapled 88-page booklet to the membership of Mt. Pisgah three weeks before the big vote. The front cover was of plain white cardstock to add emphasis to the two provocative words that were in all caps and in a bold font, "Venal Dogmata."

Dr. Lewis was throwing down the gauntlet, and Luca could not have been prouder of his father. He was going to make it clear to everyone at Mt. Pisgah Baptist that the choice that they would be making was not simply one of ceremonial preference but was in fact one of spiritual direction—one of light or of darkness. We would exist for ourselves or we would exist for our King's mission. But there could be no middle ground.

It was, after all, a choice of kingdoms.

Ironically, the pastor's selection of the two Latin words—*Venal* and *Dogmata*—was his way of not being unclear, of not being misunderstood or mistaken. *Venal* was chosen because it spoke to the concept of being for sale, or open and willing to be used for corruptive purposes. Much like the crooked politicians with their grubby hands out to the lobbyists who frequent their offices in search of favors, the church was complicit in an ecclesiological corruption. From the Lewis's perspective much about the North American version of Jesus' Way had been sold and replaced with a more convenient version. It was a *venal* transaction designed to enrich a few and lay waste to many. And it would end once and for all, at least in their neighborhood.

Dogmata was simply the plural form of dogma. If a dogma was a belief, dogmata was its overarching system. It was the structural scheme that perpetuated a belief. Put together, Luca's father was stating without equivocation that deciding with Marcus E. Robinson—the charismatic spokesman for the status quo—was not a decision of neutrality. There is no neutrality when following Christ—we are either for him or we are against him. We are never undecided. We could continue to pretend to be Jesus' church and, in the comfort of our own sanctuary, amuse ourselves into oblivion, or we could actually become Jesus' church—and courageously bring the gospel to a city where it's so desperately needed.

"Jesus has a mission," Dr. Lewis pronounced with the conviction of an Old Testament prophet, "But does he have a church for that mission? Will Mt. Pisgah Baptist Church be his church for his mission? It means very little to me whether his mission harmonizes with your inclinations, preferences, or sensibilities! I am past the point of being concerned about such trivialities. I will answer to my King personally for my obedience. And so will you."

To the seasoned Dr. Lewis, this was not the time to play religious footsie, for the stakes could not be higher. And so he'd told them in such a way that they might stay told.

At least he had hoped.

CHAPTER 8

Wednesday

WEDNESDAY ARRIVED, AND Santiago, as was his custom, sat in the second row on the very last chair on the right-hand side. Campbell McKay, sitting next to him, was shuffling through a three-ring notebook studying pages of handwritten loose-leaf outreach reports.

The black plastic chairs in the main room were completely full, and the wooden chairs in the side rooms were lined up in a perpendicular fashion resembling box seating at a stadium. They too were full. The empty floor area at the front had spilled over with a dozen or so teenagers sitting cross-legged—most holding paper cups of coffee. A couple dozen more, mostly younger men, were standing at the back by the large stainless steel coffee urns. The place was buzzing with excitement. There was a cacophony of happy sounds all merging together in Philadelphia Freedom's big room, which these days felt much too small. There was laughter, camaraderie, and a remarkable sense of enthusiasm. This was certainly the happiest place in Philly.

The room grew quiet as Big Luca, looking every day his six-plus-decades old, picked his way rather ungracefully through the tangle of chairs, legs, and backpacks as he made a circuitous path to the front. Clearing his voice and with a wide smile, he said, "How are you all doing? Or maybe I should say, Happy New Year!"

There was a thunderous cheer and a wave of high fives offered generously throughout the big room. "All right, all right, looks like you're ready for 2050, am I correct?" Luca asked somewhat rhetorically with a twinkle in his eye.

After the hooting and hollering diminished, Luca voiced, "Tell you what, I love the Wednesday crowd. Y'all aren't the most well-behaved group— but you certainly are the most fun!" More hoots and whistles were the only possible reaction to that. And they came.

"Okay, all right, Center City and South Philly, we got some stuff to take care of," Big Luca said with his most serious voice. The room immediately quieted down out of an obvious sense of respect for the man at the front.

Big Luca was no ordinary man.

CHAPTER 9

The Apprentices

THE MAIN CAMPUS of the Children's
Hospital of Philadelphia smelled like popcorn.

Noticing the aroma and popcorn cart,
Campbell McKay nodded sharply in approval.
The most powerful trigger of memory is our sense
of smell, and popcorn is never associated with bad
things. It reminds us of the movies we love, of the
circus, of parties and time with friends, of days
spent with family, and of wonder and fun. It was
a brilliant and stark counterpoint to the fear and
uncertainty of a children's hospital.

His eyes instinctively scanned the room,
taking in everything all at once: second shift,
lunch served, Jenny's haircut, Margaret seems to
be missing, Dr. Thomas's back hunch. He nodded
to Sophia, his 15-year-old apprentice, and she in
turn nodded to Ava and Anna, her fiery-haired
lieutenants. They were on a mission.

Campbell examined his team. Today it was comprised of his 12-year-old twin daughters, Sophia, the precocious daughter of his old friend, Santiago, and two new recruits in training. Tony was actually Big Luca's grandson from his youngest son, Sanders. He was tall and lean and an athletic 18-year-old who seemed a decade or two older than his years. Tony was preparing to lead a Missional Community of his own, and three months shadowing Campbell was the final part of his development plan. It seemed obvious to most that Tony's future impact on the movement was going to be substantial.

And then there was Rhonda, or "Rhonny," which was her preferred alias. She was an only child raised by a single mother who worked extra shifts at a jewelry store to put her through community college. Now a social worker in her mid-twenties, she had an empathy for hurting people that seemed both effortless and endless.

"Ready Rhonny?" Campbell asked. "You bet!" she answered without a moment of hesitation. Rhonda thrived in moments like this.

She thought to herself that it was a place just like this where her life was turned upside-right a handful of years before. Her thoughts drifted back to the University of Penn Hospital, where she held vigil watching her dear mother Brenda slowly succumb to pancreatic cancer: the light in her eyes, the deep hope in the midst of immeasurable suffering and pain, and how the visits from Luca Lewis made such a difference. It was from those divinely appointed visits that her mama's hope moved naturally into her own heart. Her mother often told the story of the affable customer who wandered into Patterson's Jewelers that fateful day in search of a cross necklace—and how that visit started a friendship that changed the trajectory of her entire life story.

Now here she was ministering in a hospital with Luca's grandson. "May God use us today like he did with Big Luca at Penn Hospital," she instinctively whispered.

Campbell McKay's heart was both full and overwhelmed at once. Glancing back and smiling, he took a deep breath.

"Réidh?" Campbell asked, not looking back this time.

"Réidh Daidí!" The redheads said playfully, and Ava handed Campbell a large paper bag.

"Wait, you're teaching them Irish?" Rhonny shook her head. "When did that start?"

Campbell was giving the room one last look to double check his plan of attack. "Right before they were born lass, right before they were born."

"Jenny!" he said, opening his arms. "I've brought you the finest blueberry muffin in the whole of Philly!"

Jenny held him with a level glance, "You religious nuts are as crazy as you are charming, Campbell. But for the sake of incoming snacks and ongoing good relations, I'll let it slide this time." Jenny took the muffin slowly, as if it were treasure, and carefully placed it in a drawer to the left of her chair.

Campbell went from winsome to solemn in the space of a heartbeat. "Sadly Jenny, 'tis a muffin of mourning. I'm grieving the loss of your long hair. You really should consult my council before any major life changes," he said with a twinkle in his eye.

Jenny tilted her head, "'Locks of Love,' my friend. But if you wanted to visit my hair, she's in room 104 battling acute lymphocytic leukemia. I had to do something."

Campbell's eyes filled with tears. He nodded to Jenny and tapped his hand on his heart and said softly, "Aw, Jenny, I can see pieces of my God's heart in your sweet spirit. I, for one, am so thankful for how well you love the sweet children here. May he bless you like crazy, my friend. May your journey of love and care and affection take you straight to its founding Source—Jesus himself."

Jenny's features softened for a brief moment, but then quickly went nurse professional again and shooed him toward the hallway, "Thank for the muffin. Now go away. I have work to . . . ."

"Miss Jenny, did you know that I was born in this hospital?" Sophia interrupted the backpedaling nurse. "Well, not actually born here—I was born in some other hospital, but I had heart surgery right here when I was a little baby."

"No, I didn't love," Jenny replied. "And it looks like all went well?" she asked. "Absolutely, Miss Jenny. Our movement, Philadelphia Freedom, arranged for everything—and paid for everything—even though they hardly knew my parents."

Jenny leaned back in her chair again and began to chew on the nib of her pen as she mumbled, "Is that a fact?"

"Oh yes, Miss Jenny. And my daddy says that this is the finest hospital in the world. Look at me now!" Sophia exclaimed as she raised her arms in the air and twirled in a circle as if she were a ballerina.

"Well, who can argue with that," the nurse responded with a warm smile. "You're certainly good advertising for us."

"Oh, yes. Between this hospital and my friends at Philadelphia Freedom, my Savior Jesus Christ did an amazing thing. So thank you, Miss Jenny, for what you do. We can all tell that it is more than just a job to you," Sophia said, never taking her eyes off of Jenny.

"And your lovely new hairstyle is living testimony to Sophia's true words," Campbell added. "The way that you carry out your sacred calling, 'tis a spiritual thing indeed."

The Irishman stopped for a brief moment, looked toward Sophia, then gazed back at the nurse who now had tears running down her flushed cheeks. Campbell spoke softly, "Jenny, my prayer for you will be, that before too long, you will know the full measure of the love of Jesus Christ. Personally. Your love for others needs a Source that can sustain you Jenny. And Jesus is that supply. He can fill you with himself so that you can be free to be the beautiful, serving, godly woman that you aspire to be. That will be my prayer for you, Jenny. That you will know Jesus' love and forgiveness just like a ol' Irish brawler like me has come to experience."

"That would be lovely," Jenny said muffled through a very moist tissue. "Thank you."

"No, thank you, Jenny. Thank you. We shall talk more later."

Campbell turned toward the patient rooms. Sophia noticed Jenny regarding Campbell with a quick look and a small upturned smile as she discreetly dabbed her dribbling mascara with a fresh tissue.

Dr. Thomas shook Campbell's hand firmly, "Good to see you, my friend, and it's wonderful to see that you brought my favorite girls and my favorite pastry," he said warmly. "This is a good day indeed."

Campbell returned the handshake and touched the old doctor's shoulder: "And you. Yes, yes, the girls keep me on the straight and narrow. Hey, is Margaret okay? I didn't see her at the desk . . . ."

Dr. Thomas lifted an eyebrow, "Oh. She's fine, her cousin is getting married in New York, so she took the train over for a few days with family. It's tough to manage without her . . . ."

Sophia jumped in unexpectedly once again, "Dr. Thomas? Is your back still bothering you?"

Dr. Thomas looked pained, "Honestly? Yes, but it's just old age, I'm afraid. Not much to be done at this point." Campbell smiled to himself thinking, *She noticed and took action with no prompting from me. Oh, that was well done, Padawan. First Jenny, now Dr. Thomas.*

Without missing a beat, Ava said, "Aw Dr. Thomas, you're not that old. My *maimeó* is old. She's all wrinkly, and you're not. Can we pray for your back?" As she did, Anna flanked the old doctor on his opposite side and nodded her approval.

Dr. Thomas laughed and looked uncomfortable all at once, "Um, I'm not sure I believe much in prayer, young Ava . . . ."

"That's okay," as she cut him off in mid-protest. "Anna and I believe enough to cover for your part too."

Dr. Thomas smiled a smile of surprise in spite of himself and, in a magical moment, slumped over in a waiting room chair and found himself surrounded by love, concern, the brief and earnest prayers of a child, and the wonder of a sense of the power of true faith that he envied and yet couldn't explain.

Room 104 got the treatment as well: kindness, laughter, genuine concern, prayer, and the outshining of the Holy Spirit. Real people touching real people in real life.

The debrief of the day's events took place, as usual, over coffees and bubble teas at Sammy's Roastery. Tony and Rhonny had already headed home when Sophia voiced her frustration in a somewhat incoherent fashion.

Campbell, growing increasingly confused, was slightly defensive in his reply: "Things are going incredibly well, Sophia. Our team is connecting people to God in Philly on a daily basis. I couldn't be prouder of you."

"You're not hearing me," said Sophia, "Of course we're doing good work." She gestured to him, to herself, to the McKay sister lieutenants, "We're good at this. This is how God made us, it's easy for us to connect. But we have another angle to cover here as well.

"Daddiago says that Evangelist is an equipping gift. And he's right. That means our role has two hands. On one hand, we do our thing and watch God blow it up. On the other hand, we help people who are scared of talking to people do it better."

"Daddiago?" asked Campbell. Wow. No one could spoof Santiago like his own daughter could.

Sophia grinned like a fox. "We're trying it out. I have to tease him to keep him from being too serious. You know how teachers can be. It's a free public service that I offer. But stop distracting me . . . .

"It's not that other people are terrible at it. They just don't see it quite right. We can help them adjust and look for God's opportunities better. If we widen our scope of training and mentoring, we can help people participate in what God is doing even more . . . ."

His freckled daughters readily nodded their red heads in solidarity.

"You're so right, girls!" Campbell exclaimed, his eyes beaming in delight. "And why do you think that Tony and Rhonny were with us today? Did we need extra help lugging around those fine blueberry muffins?" Campbell took a big sip of his coffee while he waited for a response.

"Well, they are so old," Sophia offered—a few decibels more serene than her previous pronouncement. "I thought that those two would have had this down by now."

He lovingly smiled, and then in one breath, Campbell the evangelist transformed into Campbell the shepherd/teacher as he tenderly guided his young team to a more complete understanding of the nature of the Body of Christ.

"So we all start at different places with different strengths, but our goal is to become more like the full picture of Jesus," Anna stated as she attempted to all at once summarize and internalize what her dad had just taught them.

But before Campbell could comment, Sophia blurted, "That means my shepherding IQ needs some work, because I have no patience for stupid people. They're such a pain."

"Perhaps," Campbell chortled unexpectedly, choking on a half-swallowed sip of coffee. "Just perhaps."

An excited Campbell McKay took "Daddiago" to breakfast the very next morning. This just couldn't wait.

CHAPTER 10

The Sting

THE DEMISE OF Mt. Pisgah Baptist Church was particularly hard on Dr. Lewis. His once optimistic and vibrant spirit departed in three powerful yet distinct waves.

First, it was the Marcus E. Robinson scuffle that ultimately declared God's will to be convenient, yet substantive Sunday services— but really nothing more. About one third of the congregation, "The only ones worth their salt," he used to say to Luca, left Mt. Pisgah for greener pastures. They loved Pastor Lewis, but they could not abide what went down.

The second wave wasn't actually a defined singular event but more of a sustained percussion of body blows aimed directly at his already beaten soul. Dr. Lewis was left with the unenviable assignment of shepherding a church full of sheep who could do nothing but find faults. There seemed to be almost nothing that Pastor Lewis could do right. Week-by-week Luca could see his father age before his very eyes.

The last ounce of spirit remaining in Pastor Lewis's soul drained out the day the developers of Liberty Village changed the locks on the church doors. Pastor Lewis, acquiescing that his life and ministry had been reduced to this ill-fated moment, completely and utterly broke down. Slumped over in his idling Chevy, he sobbed uncontrollably in his old familiar parking space.

And then he grew quiet.

No one found Pastor Lewis until the next morning.

The "home going" service for the late Dr. Josiah Lewis was held the following Tuesday at East Mt. Zion Korean Baptist Church. The coroner's report, which had arrived the previous day, found the death to be "of natural causes." Pastor Lewis, who had no history of heart disease, had nonetheless expired from a myocardial infarction. A massive heart attack culminating from his final dispiriting years of a broken and disheartening ministry. He was finally at rest.

The crowd wasn't small, but yet again it wasn't as large as one would suppose, given that the man of honor had served this community his entire adult life. Flowers, as expected, were arranged both at center stage by the casket and at the back foyer surrounding the guest book. Several framed photographs of Pastor Lewis were tastefully displayed below the floral array. Most were photos of Dr. Lewis looking the younger firebrand that few in this assembly would remember. There was a faded wedding portrait of him and Estelle, the love of his life who had passed away seven years previously. But it was the family picture of mom and dad and an eight- or nine-year-old version of himself from which Luca could not divert his eyes.

Luca was overcome. He was an emotional muddle of sadness, anger, loneliness, and more anger. But then a new sensation gripped him. Grinning at his own father's funeral seemed especially inappropriate to Luca—but all of a sudden, he really wanted to. He knew that his dad would have appreciated what was about to go down.

And he couldn't wait.

The Reverend Jin Soo Park, pastor of the East Mt. Zion Korean Baptist Church, conducted the event in a polished and dignified way. There was a final congregational hymn of "Blessed Assurance," special music by a family friend, and then the grand finale.

Sister Shanice Johnson carefully climbed the seven red carpeted steps, each symbolically representing the seven stations of the cross, and then stood atop the platform in front of the remains of Pastor Lewis. She offered a few sympathetic comments as the Hammond organ played wistfully in the background. As she let loose her first note of "Take my Hand Precious Lord," four young men dressed in dark suits rose to their feet, as if on cue, and unobtrusively made their way to the front row, each carrying a cardboard box branded "RightWay Printing Inc."

Sister Shanice, who appeared completely unphased by the distraction, continued to hit the high notes, one after the next, with skillful precision, despite the goings-on. The four young men worked their way down the aisles distributing the contents of their boxes to all in attendance one row at a time. And as if it had been rehearsed a dozen times before, the four young men completed their operation and reconvened in the back foyer by the guest book at the very moment that the Hammond organ faded into silence.

The gathered congregation quietly and respectfully made their way out through the front doors of East Mt. Zion Korean Baptist Church. There were some tears, to be sure. Many lingered outside the front steps catching up and sharing their opinions on the service. Most seemed quite pleased.

Most, but not all.

Marching impudently through and almost over the crowd and making a blustering beeline to his black Lexus was a seething Marcus E. Robinson. With a white-knuckled right hand he clutched the freshly printed and bound copy of the only book that the late Dr. Josiah Lewis had ever authored.

Published posthumously.

Embossed in gold lettering set against a matte black cover were the familiar yet condemning words, "Venal Dogmata."

CHAPTER 11

The Wednesday Gang

BEFORE HE GOT things started, Luca stood quietly at the back of the room, observing the friendly and relaxed banter of the people whom he called the Wednesday Gang, although the official name of this weekly event was the Center City and South Philly Regional Gathering. Each weekday, and Saturday too, the Philadelphia Freedom Center hosted three distinct groups of people from each of the 12 major regions of Philadelphia: two regions per day, Sundays off.

He smiled as he heard a guffaw of laughter from one of his comrades who held the position of "Regional Leader." *What a great group*, he thought. He was so thankful for the way the Regional Leaders got along with the Missional Pastors, and the new believers always seemed to be relaxed and enjoying themselves.

To Luca, Regional Leaders represented the healthy functioning of a holistic gospel

movement. There was a Lead Missionary, who
kept things moving forward and outward. There
was a Lead Prophet, who kept things honest—
both in theology and in alignment with the
overall vision of the movement. There was a Lead
Evangelist, who led the charge in engaging lost
communities. A Lead Shepherd ensured that
the pastoral care needs of the mission force were
being met, and a Lead Teacher coordinated the
equipping of the Missional Pastors. Luca was
grateful for these five leaders who served as a
leadership team for this region. This team visited
the scattered Missional Communities and each
member of the team took turns teaching at the
weekly Regional Gathering, like one of them
would today.

As the City Missionary, Lucas had the
privilege of getting together once a month with
these five Regional Leaders in another meeting,
along with their respective counterparts from
the other five city regions. The purpose of this
"Coordinating Meeting" was to inspire greater
accountability and movement synergy, as well
as to aid in their own personal development.
Leading and developing the Regional Leaders
with Luca at the City Movement level were
four others—again, Luca as City Missionary,

along with a City Prophet, City Evangelist, City Shepherd, and City Teacher.

It was time to get started. He watched as Bernie, a usually introverted and cerebral Missional Pastor, telling some sort of impassioned story to several others gathered around. *Bernie?* he thought to himself, *Now that is a sight to see!*

Bernie, along with the nearly 90 other Missional Pastors included in the Wednesday Gang, took the lead in ensuring that their local Missional Communities were a fully functioning expression of Christ's body in a neighborhood. Luca always took great satisfaction in hearing the reports of how these leaders took spiritual responsibility for their geography. They were the lifeblood of Philadelphia Freedom, bringing the gospel of Jesus into every place imaginable. It was such a crucial role that Luca required that both the Regional Leaders and the City Movement Leaders stayed fresh by serving as Missional Pastors themselves.

As Luca picked his way to the front, his eyes were scanning the big room for Francisco. Well, actually he was looking for a brand-new believer named Melanie, who was likely close by Francisco. Before things got going, he wanted to pray with Melanie. Francisco, her Missional

Pastor, had called Luca earlier in the week, mentioning that Melanie's sister was in cancer treatment, and things were not looking good. Luca, with one giant hand on Francisco's shoulder and the other on Melanie's, interceded with unwavering conviction for his new sister's sister.

Melanie and 21 others were at this week's Regional Gathering because they had recently repented of their sins and submitted their lives to the lordship of Jesus. The week following their baptisms, new believers were invited to attend the Regional Gathering to be introduced to the larger community by their Missional Pastor. This was always the highlight of Luca's day.

"All right, then." Luca looked down at his notes, and the group began to break up their conversations and find their seats. His plan didn't vary much from meeting to meeting. After an opening prayer, there would be neighborhood huddles in the breakout rooms. They would talk about events being planned in all the neighborhoods throughout their Region. Then, there would be an equipping time led by one of their Regional Leaders. They'd finish up with celebration time, when they'd hear the stories of those who had recently come to Christ. "Okay, Wednesday Gang. So good to see you again. Let's thank the Lord for his guidance tonight . . . and let's get after it!"

A few minutes later, as the people he'd come to love so much headed to their breakout rooms, he took a moment to breathe a prayer for wisdom once again—wisdom from Jesus, wisdom for himself, wisdom for all. The vision had been cast and it was taking hold. At the end of every meeting, he'd hear comments about how excited they were, what a privilege it was to be a part of what God was doing in their communities. He went home most nights on cloud nine.

Tonight was going to be no exception.

———

A lot had happened over the past 25 years. It all started with a simple four-point manifesto, ideas taken from the book Luca had published at RightWay Printing in West Philly for his dad's home going. From there, Luca had reduced his dad's more lofty and philosophical thoughts to four memorable and actionable ideas.

He called it, in honor of his late father, "*The Venal Dogmata Manifesto.*"

It was simply a one-page document that started with a single paragraph of introduction describing the manifesto's purpose. And from there it got to business. It only had four points, each with a paragraph of explanation.

As simple and unassuming as it was, this guiding document had unleashed a spiritual renewal that the city had not seen since the Second Great Awakening.

The four revolutionary ideas were:

1. We meet people where they live—not ask them to search for us.
2. The gospel is everyone's vocation—not just a chosen few.
3. The church is the functioning body of Christ in community—not a Sunday service.
4. The kingdom of God is our only goal—not the advancement of our brand.

It all started with a younger, thinner Luca Lewis, four other faith-filled friends, and a firm resolve to allow Jesus Christ to demonstrate his great power through their yielded weakness. In that spirit of surrender they unleashed the words and passions of Dr. Josiah Lewis and watched them multiply into a movement that nobody saw coming.

CHAPTER 12

The Doorman's Prayer

WEDNESDAY WAS HERE, and Santiago was ready—nervous but ready. Hunched on the second row and anxiously bouncing his left knee as if Sophia needed amusing, his thoughts drifted to four years previous, when he was still a schoolteacher and was dealing hopelessly with news of his baby girl's health. A lot has happened since then. Much because of that big man who is speaking right now.

Santiago instinctively offered a prayer of praise as Luca waxed eloquently on future multiplication plans for the Philadelphia Freedom network: "Thank you, Father," Santiago breathed, "For the life that you have given me. For the journey. I do not deserve these blessings—and I am oh so grateful. Please give me your words and your heart to convey courage and encouragement to these remarkable brothers and sisters . . . ."

As Santiago was deep in reflection, he heard Luca mention his name.

" . . . and so I brought perogies to that Chilean's apartment, and he called me an African Ukrainian!" He laughed just as hard as he had the first time. "We had a wonderful time celebrating New Year's. I love this brother. I know that you do too."

The room roared in affirmation. "Brothers and sisters, it's a new year and a new decade, why don't we ask our Teaching Director to come and remind us of something old. Come on up, brother."

The room once again erupted in applause. Santiago quickly rose to his feet and strode deliberately to the podium. This was why Santiago was put on this earth. This was his mission. He would gladly trade being a schoolteacher and working a thousand years as a doorman if he was allowed to encourage these courageous kingdom warriors just one more time.

With a gentle spirit paradoxically wedded to an uncommon sense of personal conviction, Santiago began to teach: "Thank you, Brother Luca. Words cannot express my gratitude to be counted among this number and to have this opportunity to serve you this evening. Over the next four Wednesdays we are going to make very practical the four tenets of our Manifesto—what it means to be a part of the Philadelphia Freedom family. We are going to dig into Scripture and see how significant these concepts are for the advancement of our King's commission. So tonight we will begin with the kingdom obligation of inconveniencing ourselves, in order to bring the gospel to where it is needed the most . . . ."

Big Luca couldn't help but watch Santiago so simply unfold the Scriptures with a sense of fatherly pride. It was only for a minute, and then Luca too found himself offering a heartfelt prayer of praise to his heavenly Father, "Oh God, what an undeserved blessing this is . . . ."

CHAPTER 13

Irish Empanadas

IT WAS ALMOST midnight and the aroma of empanadas and green curry still lingered in the cozy Belfast flat. The bubbly 24-year-old host, an extroverted "fill the room" kind of personality, was in mid-sentence telling one of her most embarrassing moments when Tony, the Global Missions Director, uttered:

"Shhh, everyone, it's almost time!"

"Oh, Tony, you're so much like your papa, maybe even more so! You're a mini-Sanders 2.0, sans the computer skills!" she laughingly replied. "But I know that he's proud of you. We all are, Tony." Her gaze turned upwards as her spirit quickly quieted, with misty eyes she struggled, "And your grandpa Luca," she continued slowly, "he would have been so proud to see all the places that you've brought the Philly network."

The small flat erupted in unison with a spontaneous yet deeply heartfelt "Amen." What a ride it had been. And it was far from over.

The most senior member in the room stood, hoisted his glass of sparkling water in the air, and led them in a toast, "And may God use this rag-tag apostolic team, like he has used so many others who have left our City of Brotherly Love, to unleash a Jesus movement in this beautiful country. A Jesus movement that will complete the lives of the most unlikely and desperate people. Desperate and unlikely people like myself. May he use us. May he use all of us."

A thunderous "Amen" filled the flat as friends soaked in the moment.

Then the white-haired man, who appeared to be in his mid-seventies, lowered his glass, cleared his throat as his moist, grey eyes gazed at the ceiling, and in a faltering voice, stammered, "And . . . may God even use . . . an old sawbones . . . like me."

There was a keen sense of anticipation on this late Tuesday evening—not because these friends were so euphoric to see the Belfast fireworks, but because it was a new year, actually a new decade. The spiritual family in this flat were all leaders in a new missional network that was taking off in

Ireland. So much was ahead of them—and almost all of it unknown.

But the unknown was actually familiar in an odd sort of way—it was the spiritual adventure they had been taught to live. It was the very space where they thrived. It truly seemed to be the only place where they experienced, first-hand, the power of their King. So they were good with the unknown—to this band of brothers and sisters, it was home turf.

Even the ring of the new year seemed unknown. It was going to take a minute to learn to naturally say 2070. Especially tweaking a South Philly accent into a Northern Irish lilt.

But Sophia and her friends were up for the challenge. So too were the McKay sisters.

But for the spry, tall, and energetic Dr. Thomas, this would be entirely new.

Venal Dogmata
Three-Session
Conversation Guide

Notes to Group Leaders:

The following conversations are designed to provide opportunities for participants to make new discoveries about God, their communities, and themselves. We pray God will inspire new obedience individually and in groups that will result in a Jesus movement across North America.

Here are five tips to get the most out of these conversations.

1. Pray that the Holy Spirit would move in the hearts and minds of each person, providing new convictions about next steps.
2. Take the role as facilitator and coach. Let God use parable to teach. Encourage discussions and help the group imagine new possibilities for influencing people for Christ. Resist the

temptation to do all the talking. Listen well and keep asking.

3. Ensure everyone gets an opportunity to contribute to the conversation. Create a rhythm that involves calling people by name to get their insights. Cheer them along by making affirming comments about responses to questions.

4. Encourage participants to reflect on questions, one at a time, and write short answers. Discuss the answers. Then, move to the next question.

5. If possible, use a wall poster or dry erase board to display answers to questions that require brainstorming.

Venal Dogmata Conversation #1 (pp. 21-33)

I therefore, a prisoner for the Lord, urge you to walk in a manner worthy of the calling to which you have been called (Eph. 4:1).

> *But there was something else. It wasn't what they did, or what they said necessarily—it was the way they did it. Their eyes didn't say pity as much as they said compassion—or love. And it was obvious, as Santiago and Maggy invited these strangers into their apartment, that these*

> *large-hearted people were their neighbors—not*
> *the richy-rich types from Liberty Village Lofts.*
> *These generous gifts of love were given from*
> *working people who were no better off than*
> *they were* (*Venal Dogmata*, 31).

- What hurting people in your community present opportunities for gospel ministry?
- What opportunity merits further prayer and investigation?
- What people in your community are typically treated as "inferior" by Christians?
- What causes churches or groups to lose their relevancy?
- What did you feel as you read about "Philadelphia Freedom" and the vision of Luca Lewis?
- How can your church or group multiply new spiritual communities in order to help reach new people with the gospel?
- What will your church or group look like in 2050?
- Use your kingdom imagination: What will a life-giving, relevant church look like in 2050?

Venal Dogmata Conversation #2 (pp. 35-59)

And he gave the apostles, the prophets, the evangelists, the shepherds and teachers, to equip the saints for the work of ministry, for building up the body of Christ, until we all attain to the unity of the faith and of the knowledge of the Son of God, to mature manhood, to the measure of the stature of the fullness of Christ (Eph. 4:11-12 ESV)

> *The first floor's grand hallway was lined with ministries designed to meet the needs of Philadelphia's most vulnerable. Each one with signage and environments that declared that they were putting their very best foot forward. It was always abuzz with grateful immigrants from around the globe, recovering addicts of assorted dependencies, desperate single mothers, and adult students eager for a fresh start by learning critical life skills* (Venal Dogmata, 41).

- What is the most important "first floor" activity initiated by your church or group for people in your community?

- What "second floor" engagements with local businesses can result in the good of your community?
- What intentional "third floor" equipping is being done to multiply disciple-makers?
- What story of life change in your world is most encouraging?
- What person who is far from God but close to you needs more of your attention?
- Which of Luca's "spiritual disorders" is most obvious in your church or group?
- What steps can you take to recover?
- What was happening inside of you when you read Dr. Josiah Lewis's sermon?

Venal Dogmata Conversation #3 (pp. 61-97)

Rather, speaking the truth in love, we are to grow up in every way into him who is the head, into Christ, from whom the whole body, joined and held together by every joint with which it is equipped, when each part is working properly, makes the body grow so that it builds itself up in love (Eph. 4:15-16 ESV).

> *To Luca, Regional Leaders represented the healthy functioning of a holistic gospel movement. There was a Lead Missionary, who*

> *kept things moving forward and outward.*
> *There was a Lead Prophet who kept things*
> *honest—both in theology and in alignment*
> *with the overall vision of the movement. There*
> *was a Lead Evangelist, who led the charge in*
> *engaging lost communities. A Lead Shepherd*
> *ensured that the pastoral care needs of the*
> *mission force were being met, and a Lead*
> *Teacher coordinated the equipping of the*
> *Missional Pastors* (*Venal Dogmata*, 85).

- What groups in your community are totally unaware of the true Christian message?
- What people in the spaces that you are already going to need more attention from you?
- How can you engage them more personally over the next two weeks?
- Which insights did you gain from reading Luca's "four revolutionary ideas"?
- What does God want to change about your church or group?
- What have you learned about yourself from reading this parable?
- What is God saying?
- How does obedience to Christ look for you now?

About the Author

JEFF CHRISTOPHERSON @christopherson3 is Co-Founder and Missiologist of the Send Institute—an interdenominational church planting think-tank. He is the author of several books, including *Kingdom Matrix: Designing a Church for the Kingdom of God* and *Kingdom First: Starting Churches that Shape Movements*. He also writes as a weekly columnist in *Christianity Today* with *Missio Mondays*. Jeff serves as a co-vocational pastor of The Sanctuary in Oakville, Ontario. He is married to Laura and has two married children.